The King's Clocks

Written by Patricia McGinn
Illustrated by Damon J. Taylor

There was a big round clock in the castle tower, a grandfather clock in the entryway, and a grandmother clock in the corner of the library.

A mantle clock was centered over the fireplace.

There were wall clocks in the kitchen, cuckoo clocks in the castle hallways, and clocks of all shapes and sizes on desks and tables everywhere.

The castle clicked with the tick-tock, tick-tock, tick-tock of all the King's clocks. On the hour the clocks sounded together in a great chorus. BONG, BONG, BONG pealed the tower clock. GONG, GONG, GONG struck the grandfather clock. Chime, chime, chime rang the grandmother clock. Cuckoo, cuckoo, cuckoo went the cuckoo clocks. Ring, ding, dong, RATTLE, BANG, CLANG tolled the others.

The King lived his life by his clocks. At 7 o'clock in the morning, not 6:30 or 7:15, but at 7 o'clock exactly, his bedside clock rang, and he sat straight up in bed.

"It must be time to get up," he thought to himself. "The clock says 7 o'clock, and I always get up at 7 o'clock."

So, although he wasn't fully rested, he rolled out of bed and fell over when he reached for his slippers.

He nicked himself while shaving... and forgot to put in his false teeth.

At 8 o'clock in the morning, not 7:30 or 8:15, but at 8 o'clock exactly, he sat at the royal table. "It must be time to eat," he thought to himself. "The clock says 8 o'clock, and I always eat breakfast at 8 o'clock."

So, although he wasn't very hungry, he ate all the eggs, sausage, toast, jam, potatoes, and muffins he was served simply because it was time to eat.

Before long he began to gain weight. His royal belt needed another hole, and the tailor had to fit him with tently robes.

At 9 o'clock in the morning, not 8:30 or 9:15, but at 9 o'clock exactly, he went into the royal library. He sat in his red leather chair behind his king-size desk. "It must be time to write a proclamation," he thought to himself. "The clock says 9 o'clock, and I always write proclamations at 9 o'clock."

So, although he didn't have anything important to proclaim, he made up something.

He once proclaimed that all the clocks in the kingdom be wound and oiled at 2 o'clock on the first and third Friday of each month.

The villagers were annoyed when they had to interrupt their work, housekeeping, and studies to wind and oil the clocks.

Another time he proclaimed that all the windows in the village be washed at 10 o'clock on the third Thursday of the month.

As it happened, it rained on the third Thursday. The villagers were annoyed when they went out in their raincoats, raincaps, and galoshes to wash windows.

At 10 o'clock in the morning, not 9:30 or 10:15, but at 10 o'clock exactly, the King took a walk in the royal rose garden and fed the birds. "It must be time to walk in the garden," he thought to himself. "The clock says 10 o'clock, and I always take my walk at 10 o'clock."

So, although the roses had been pruned back and the birds had flown south for the winter, he went for a walk. He caught a cold and sneezed for days.

At 11 o'clock in the morning, not 10:30 or 11:15, but at 11 o'clock exactly, he received visitors. He met with a duke, an earl, and a prince until noon. Although they were not finished with their visit and had come quite a long distance, they had to leave because it was time for the King's lunch.

He started to get a reputation for being rude and unfriendly. Fewer and fewer visitors came to visit until no one came at all.

The King's afternoon and evening ran as precisely as his clocks. Everything he did was at a set time. Oddly enough, he never seemed to have enough time. He had not been into the village in months, and he missed his subjects.

He missed the Queen too. He rarely saw her anymore. They once loved going out in the royal carriage, but it sat gathering dust in the royal stable.

"I don't have any fun anymore," thought the King. "I need more time."

"I will get another clock; perhaps that will help."

And so yet another clock joined the great chorus in the castle. Of course, it didn't help.

One day all the clocks stopped. When the King awoke, the castle was quiet. Not a tick or a tock was heard. "I must have overslept," he thought as he sat up and stretched. "I do feel well rested. I wonder if it is time to get up?"

He called for his servant. "What time is it?" he asked the servant.

"I don't know, sire," replied the servant. "All of the castle clocks have stopped."

"Oh my," said the King. "How will I know if it is time to get up?"

The King called the Queen. "My dear, do you know the time?" he asked.

"No, dearest," she replied, "all of the clocks have stopped."

"Oh my," said the King, "this is a royal problem. I don't know when to get up."

"The castle Wise-One will know," said the Queen.

And so the Wise-One was called to the King's bedside.

"Can you help me, Wise-One?" asked the King. "The clocks have all stopped. Do you know if it is time for me to get up?"

"Of course," replied the Wise-One. "But first, tell me, are you well rested?"

"Yes," said the King. "I must have overslept. I feel great."

"Well, then," said the Wise-One, "since you are well rested, it is time to get up."

"Good," said the King as he reached for his slippers.

He put them on without falling over. He shaved without nicking himself, and he remembered to put in his false teeth.

"Oh my," said the King, thinking about breakfast, "I don't know if it is time to eat." He called the Wise-One again.

"Can you help me again, Wise-One?" asked the King. "Do you know if it is time for me to eat?"

"Of course," replied the Wise-One. "but first tell me, are you hungry?"

"Yes," replied the King.

"Well then," said the Wise-One, "since you are hungry, it is time to eat."

"Good," said the King as he reached for a pancake.

Then he stopped and thought for a moment. "How will I know when breakfast is over?" he asked.

"Since you are hungry now," replied the Wise-One, "it is time to eat. When your hunger is satisfied, breakfast will be over."

"How clever," said the King as he buttered his toast. He ate until he was full.

I wonder if it's time to proclaim something, the king thought as he sat at his desk. He called the Wise-One again. "Do you know if it is time for me to proclaim something?" asked the King.

"Of course," said the Wise-One, "but first tell me, do you have anything necessary or helpful to proclaim?"

The King thought for a moment. "No," he replied.

"Then it is not time to make a proclamation," said the Wise-One.

"Is it time to walk in the garden?" asked the King.

"If the flowers are in bloom and the birds are singing..." said the Wise-One. The King went to the window. It was cold and dark.

"Maybe I should see visitors now instead," said the King.

"Has anyone come to visit you?" asked the Wise-One.

The King looked into the empty waiting room. "This is a royal problem," said the King. "I have no visitors, the garden is not in bloom, I have nothing to proclaim, and I don't know what time it is. What shall I do?"

"Well," said the Wise-One, "that depends—you are well rested and well fed. The day is yours, and you may do anything you like. After all, you are the King."

"You are right," said the King. "I know exactly what time it is. It is time to do whatever I like."

So he and the Queen took a ride in the royal carriage. They visited the village.

Everyone was happy to see him.

He made one proclamation. "I proclaim," he said, "since I rule the kingdom, I will no longer be ruled by my clocks."

He ate lunch when he was hungry, and after lunch he and the Queen rode to a neighboring kingdom to visit. They brought a clock as a gift.

The next day all the clocks worked again. The clock by the King's bed rang loud and long.

He sat up. "It must be time to get up," he thought to himself. "The clock says 7 o'clock, and I always get up at 7 o'clock. But should I?" he asked himself. "Am I well rested? No, I am not."

So he turned over, pulled the covers over his head, and went back to sleep.

And the sound of his snoring filled the castle.